ZOMBIE LOTTERY

By
Michelle Birbeck

Published in 2015 by Michelle Birbeck
Copyright © Michelle Birbeck, the author as named on the book cover.

First Edition

A CIP catalogue record for this title is available from the British Library.

Cover design by: © Michelle Birbeck
Cover images by: © raingizzz BigStockPhoto ID: 62530625

DEDICATION

To Chris Thurston. Thank you for distracting me with cemeteries, crazy theories on why anyone would need extra walls in one, and inadvertently giving me the experience of walking around Edinburgh whilst writing. This is what came of it.

ZOMBIE LOTTERY

At dawn, the three acre cemetery was bathed in a light fog. A lone figure ambled around the perimeter, jangling keys hanging from bony fingers. Each of four gates was locked in turn. The tall steel panels had never been designed to ward off intruders. Cemeteries had a way of doing that all on their own. Yet only on this day and night were the gates locked with such careful precision.

Visitors were always welcome. Tonight they were mandatory.

The cemetery's last gate locked with a clang, securing the interior from escapees, at least until the following dawn when only one would walk away.

"See you in two days," the old man said as he tossed the keys to the first of the night's crew members.

"Unless you lose."

The man chuckled, a dark and disturbing sound. "We all lose, son. Either I'll be in there tonight, or I'll end up there as one of them when I'm dead."

Head crew member Jack shrugged his large shoulders. "We're not far off, anyway. Couple more years and feeding them won't be enough because we won't have enough people left to feed to them."

The old man shook his head and sent up a prayer that some day the cure for this mess would be found. He knew, however, that the scientists had been working on a cure for over five years. If they hadn't found it now, they didn't have the time left to do so.

"Just be glad it's only a few that rise," he said, and waved his goodbye so he could go home to hide and pray.

Jack offered a wave in return and went to work. His crew turned up in dribbles. This was the one day of the year staff at Secure Inc. were allowed to be late. Every one of them was entered into the lottery, and the odds of winning were better every year.

"You know the drill," Jack called over his group. "Lottery winners get funnelled in through the main gate. Nothing gets out. Not until the only thing standing is the last survivor."

Solemn nods abounded, and the group headed off to complete their tasks.

Elsewhere in the town, in the grand old house that had been in the mayor's family for five generations, the names of every person alive above legal age were being put into a jar. The survivor from the previous year, whose name was back in simply because they were alive, got the job of drawing the new names. In the presence of the aging mayor and a specially selected police force, the names would be drawn, and the police would be dispatched to gather the winners.

Whole families had already been wiped out by the plague, and still no one knew which bodies would rise or how many lives would be taken this year.

When it came time to drawing the names, no one spoke. The thick silence was only broken by the sound of rustling papers, and when that was done, the heavy boots of the police leaving to collect the winners.

~***~

Zombie Lottery

In a small house at the edge of town, Sandra prepared tomato soup and sandwiches for her husband and two children. Like most houses in town, Sandra's was quiet, fear filtering into every action.

Few people worked the day the zombies rose. Essential care and those preparing for the evening were the only ones who could be torn away from their families. For shop workers like Sandra, and accountants like her husband Jim, the zombie lottery had become a national holiday. Though holiday implied joviality, and only the sadistic took joy in the death of hundreds.

Sandra served lunch in silence with the vague hint of a smile on her face. Her eyes, however, shone with unshed tears. She thought that if she forced a smile, the horrors of the day might escape her brain or at least her outward appearance. But the harder Sandra tried to smile, the more she wanted to cry.

The names would be drawn once the rising had begun, but each year more rose. Each year, more died.

And every year that passed, Sandra's children grew closer to legal age.

Once children hit eighteen it didn't matter how old they got or how able they were, they could all be chosen. Indiscriminate is what the selection process had been called. Whether people agreed or not, they all accepted their fate.

And what was the lesser of the evils? Letting the zombies roam free to kill and feed as they wanted, children included? Or choose once a year and give the scientists time to find a resolution.

Sandra shook her head and glanced around the table.

The children, Beth and Scott, ate their soup and sandwiches easily. Sandra hoped that the only worries plaguing their minds were their return to school after the day's break.

Jim, however, sat stirring his spoon around his bowl, letting a plume of steam rise from the soup.

"You need to eat," Sandra whispered, the first words of the meal.

Jim glanced at Sandra's untouched bowl and said, "So do you."

In response, she took a big spoon of soup, shovelled it into her mouth, and swallowed the tasteless liquid. It could have been the best tasting soup in the world, and Sandra wouldn't have been able to taste a thing.

No more words were spoken, the only sound the scraping of metal against pot. Their house was one of many, and all sat in silence, awaiting their fate.

The first dead rose three minutes after sunset. Jack's crew, armed with cameras, patrolled the perimeter of the cemetery maze, cataloguing the rising bodies in each section. The last dead of the night rose sixty three minutes after sunset in Jack's section. He snapped a picture, waited ten more minutes, and got on his radio.

"That's all for tonight," he told the crew. "Let's get the numbers."

The crew trudged back around the cemetery, cold ground and crispy leaves crunching under their boots. One by one, the photos were loaded onto Jack's computer. For half an hour they checked their numbers, ensuring no doubles were counted but that everyone was accounted for. Every bone that protruded from flesh was noted. Each eye that slipped in an out of the socket was identified. Every last feature, right down to the shade of puss oozing from their various wounds, was added to their lists so they didn't miscount on the night's numbers.

"Final count?" Jack asked.

Second in command, Kenny, totted up the numbers, wrote down a figure, then totted them up again. "Hundred and eighty seven. Twelve more than last year."

Someone muttered, "Thank God they don't all rise."

Another answered with, "Amen to that."

Tonight was the kind of night where everyone prayed to someone.

The first most people knew of the zombie lottery results was when an armed police officer showed up at their door to escort them out. Substitutes were not accepted, in an effort to keep the macabre dealings fair.

In Sandra's house, the dishes had been washed and put away, the table had been cleared and wiped down, and the family sat in front of a silent television. The children's hands shook as they clung to a parent each. Sandra and Jim sat straight backed and terse.

When the knock came, it had the family almost leaping out of their seats. Tears sprang up from Beth.

No one visited tonight. No one except the police carrying a death sentence.

Jim pulled away from his family and shuffled to the closed door. He unlocked it with slow, clumsy movements, hands shaking as he pulled it open. Two officers, all in black, stood in the dim outside light.

"Sandra Evans," one of the officers said.

All of Jim's blood drained down to his feet. He swayed and had to grab the door frame for support.

The officers ignored him and stomped into the house, straight into the living room. Hard faces twitched at the sight before them.

Both kids clung to their mother, tears staining their faces.

"Sandra Evans? ID please."

Sobs rose up from the children, their fingers digging into their mother's hip and waist.

"It's on the table," she told them. She couldn't bear to let go of Beth and Scott just yet. Not until she had to.

As the soldiers checked her details against their records, Sandra leaned into the warmth of her children.

"Be good for your father," she told them. "Remember that I love you. Always and forever."

Her words fizzled out, coming to a stop and letting her hard embrace take over.

Nothing she could say would make this night any better. Couldn't make it any worse, either. But that was the way of bad situations. When the tunnel you just walked into was so dark, full of so many twists and turns, that seeing to the other side wasn't possible. No amount of adjusting to the dark could let in the light at the end. And now, as Sandra was led from her home into the night, she felt that even if there was a dawn breaking around the corner, she would be too dead or blind to see it.

Throughout the town, officers collected the winners of the zombie lottery. Though when the term had first been uttered, it had been denounced as a piss poor choice of words. But doomed, dead, and chosen were equally as ill designed for the "winnings" that awaited those drawn.

Each person was checked and counted, and then bundled onto the back of a local bus commandeered for the occasion.

As the death buses, as they were affectionately known, made their rounds, people peered out of their homes. Curtains twitched, their owners praying to their gods that this not be their night. Even those who believed this plague was sign that God had abandoned them still offered up words of hope.

Anguished cries sounded in the night when the bus stopped, with whole families shaking in terror that the bus outside was there for them. The screams of relatives followed the winners out into the dark. They were but a prelude to the terrors that awaited them in the cemetery.

Jack's crew stood ever vigilant around the cemetery, awaiting the first bus. This year his crew had been spared. Not by some grand scheme of reward for the work they did every year, but by the luck of the draw. Years had come and gone when Jack wished his name came out, if only so he didn't have to play witness any longer. His nightmares left him cold and clammy near every night. Until the winners were drawn again and new nightmares took over and merged with the old ones to create a monster few saw.

Last year's winners had been the worst. An eighteen year old who had been eaten from her feet to her eyes, and Jack's own grandmother, well into her eighties, who had stumbled and broken her hip. She had laid there, rain pattering down on her face and soaking her clothes, and shivered until a zombie found her and tore out her throat in a gush of red.

Jack closed his eyes, hard, and immediately wished he hadn't. He had lost more men from his crew to nightmares and stress than to the zombies. First sign was the nightmares staying with them during the day.

Can they really be called nightmares if they come when you're awake? Jack thought.

But before he could answer that question, the radio crackled to life to announce the arrival of the first death bus.

It rattled to a stop next to the temporary holding area. A round faced driver turned off the engine before it riled up the dead. Two officers in black body armour disembarked first and stood between the bus's doors and the holding area gate.

Jack grabbed the keys off his utility belt. The door could only be opened from the outside with the single key only Jack held.

Shaking, pale faced people of all ages, shapes and sizes, piled off the bus. Some took a seat on the damp floor despite the cold. Others stood near the door, as though thoughts of escape could help them through the night.

Five years, Jack thought, *and no one's ever escaped.*

Not after Jack and his crew had been brought in before the second year of the lottery. The first year had almost been an unmitigated disaster, with people being herded into the cemetery at gunpoint. If it hadn't been for the twenty-seven person over-count that had happened, combined with all the zombies crawling back into their graves by dawn, in their cemetery alone, the powers that be might have called the whole thing off and gone back to the first couple of years of the risings. A time during which the zombies were left to run free in the cemeteries to eat whoever they wanted, or whoever got too curious for their own good. It might have been left that way, if a group of kids hadn't stumbled upon an unmarked cemetery over in some country Jack had never heard of before. Oldest one had been seven, and the incident had caused enough widespread outrage that the lottery had become reality.

Jack locked the gate behind the last of this batch of winners. Around him, the night came alive. Not with the usual nocturnal sounds of insects and night birds, but with the soft moans that rose from the walled cemetery. As the sounds of the hungry dead rose, so did the volume of sobs and desperate prayers from the winners.

Huddled in one corner of the holding area, Charlie hugged his knees and wished the zombies rose during the summer so at least his seat on the bare ground wouldn't be cold. Frantic prayers sounded from all around him and had been grating on his nerves since he boarded the bus. He ground his teeth, hugged his knees tighter, and tried to stop the shivering from setting in. His fingers were stiff as he flexed them against the cold. He flinched as he shoved the icy digits into the sleeve ends of his jumper in an attempt to warm them.

The TV told everyone every year to be prepared. Dress in warm clothes. Make sure your will is up to date. Write letters to your loved ones.

And here I am worried about not having gloves, Charlie thought.

The gates he had come through opened long enough to allow the second bus load of "winners" into the pen, causing Charlie to grind his teeth harder. He had done his praying before the lottery had been drawn. If there was a God, Charlie figured he would still be at home. So why bother asking to be spared when he had already been served up as a sacrifice. One person was getting out of this alive, and if what he had heard was anything to go by, most of those survivors did not live long enough to see another rising.

Charlie only wished everyone else thought the same way. There would be a lot more quiet and a lot less crying if they did.

"Want some company?"

Charlie looked up at a woman with long, dark hair pulled into a pony tail. She stood huddled in her coat, hands stuffed in the pockets.

"You're not trying to start a prayer circle, are you?" Charlie nodded over to a group who had joined hands and were praying in the opposite corner.

She glanced over her shoulder, then back at Charlie. "No. Don't see the point. We're all dead anyway, right?"

Charlie smiled. "Take a seat. I'm Charlie."

"Sandra."

She took a seat, pose matching Charlie's and the pair lapsed into silence, awaiting their death.

~***~

Two hours after the winners had been drawn, the doors to the holding area opened for the last time. A tunnel had been erected that formed a path from the doorway to the main gates of the cemetery.

From somewhere outside, a loud voice sounded. "Do not attempt to escape. An armed guard is situated along each side. Please make your way down the tunnel."

The instructions ended with the slight whine of a loudspeaker being turned off.

Almost two hundred pairs of feet began to shuffle forward towards the shining tunnel. A couple of people placed hands on the tunnel's sides, but quickly removed them. Those muttering prayers ceased their hopeful mumblings.

The tunnel may as well have had a sign at its entrance that read "Abandon hope all ye who enter here." Instead, there was nothing but brilliant white light and the knowledge that at the end was death.

Sandra entered the tunnel alongside Charlie. They hadn't said a word to each other since sitting down, and Sandra liked that just fine. But as people filled every space of the tunnel, she couldn't help but mutter, "I thought go into the light was reserved for the already dead?"

Charlie burst out laughing.

The sudden, joyous sound earned both Sandra and Charlie several dirty looks. Happiness, when dinner was about to be served, was apparently not appreciated. Even if the only item on the menu was human flesh and the ones eating were already dead.

Sandra smiled. "Seems jokes aren't welcome."

"Aye." Charlie leaned in close. "Doesn't mean we can't enjoy our last moments on Earth."

Sandra's smile turned into a frown. "Yeah, but I'd rather be spending them with my kids."

"How many you got?"

Zombie Lottery

The crush of people moved forward.

"Two, girl and a boy. You?"

"No. Had a sister. She's buried back home. I moved here just before they put a ban on moving."

"Too many people moving to towns with small cemeteries."

"Or bigger populations."

When the lottery became mandatory, people had done anything and everything to avoid their names being drawn. Moving from places with a twenty percent chance of winning to somewhere that had a chance of less than seven. People changed their names and never updated their ID, trying to get around the strict checks that were in place. Others went to more extreme lengths. Murder-suicides had been at an all-time high the year after the lottery came in.

Even five years later the occasional whole family would be found dead in their homes. Some of whom were only found when one or more started roaming the streets looking for flesh.

The crowd surged forward.

"Looks like it's time for dinner," Sandra said with a last look at Charlie.

All along the high walls of the sunken cemetery, people gathered to watch. Most huddled in their jackets and watched for their loved ones who had been marched out of their homes earlier in the evening. Some of the spectators, however, were there to catch a glimpse of the risen dead. But one small corner of the wall, away from everyone else, was filled with a group of morbid onlookers.

Smiles decorated their faces. Those directly in front of the wall leaned over it, pointing out the loitering dead with excited hands. There were those in that secluded group who were eligible for the lottery. Every year their names were entered into the draw, and yet

Michelle Birbeck

they still showed up at the wall with eager eyes trained on the slaughter. Their excited chatter swelled when the gates creaked open and the winners were herded into the cemetery.

Screams soon drowned out the chatter.

Charlie's whole body tightened as the first scream echoed down the packed tunnel. It would be so much quicker, he thought, if the undead were confined to a small area. The whole debacle would be over in half the time.

The powers that be had tried it, of course, but disasters didn't sell well and herding zombies was the definition of a disaster.

He turned to Sandra. "Well, I don't suppose 'nice to meet you,' is appropriate?"

"Not sure there's any such thing as inappropriate, given the circumstances."

Charlie laughed, and Sandra joined him. Only this time there were no dirty looks from those whispering prayers. All attention was on the looming gates; all ears trained to the sound of slaughter.

"Well, then, Sandra." Charlie offered her his hand. "It's been nice meeting you."

She took the offered hand and they shook.

"Nice to meet you, too, Charlie. Good luck in there."

"You, too. And thanks for not praying with me."

A gap opened up in front of Charlie and Sandra, and the crowd behind them forced them forwards. Feet shuffled along the tunnel. Those shuffles tried to turn into a rush as people fought to get out of the bottle neck at the gates. Several people behind Charlie began to push their way through the crowd. Whether they were eager for death or just wanted to get out into the maze of cemetery walls, Charlie didn't know.

He and Sandra backed away from the crushing crowd. Death would get around to them soon enough. Charlie might have given up on praying, but that wasn't the same thing as being eager for the bite of the dead. Besides, everyone knew that just because a zombie ate the body, didn't mean they killed their meal first. Rare was their preferred method of eating; rare and still screaming.

Charlie glanced down at Sandra. She seemed so much shorter than he was now they were stood next to each other. Sat down, he'd thought she was the same height.

"Want to stick together?" he asked on a whim.

She glanced up at him with narrowed eyes and pursed lips.

"I promise not to throw you to the zombies." He smiled. "You never know, you might see your kids again."

The sound that erupted from Sandra was a strangled, bitter laugh. "Yeah," she said. "I start thinking like that, I'll get myself eaten alive. And I fully intend to be dead long before my screams are etched onto people's minds."

"All right then. I promise to kill you if the zombies start at your feet," Charlie amended.

Sandra stuck out her hand. "Deal."

They shook once, and stepped forwards to the gates of hell.

Francis pulled her long, black coat tighter around her shoulders. The old jumper she wore underneath offered little extra warmth against the night air. Even her group of friends, huddled close together, generated too little heat to warm each other.

We're all just as dead as the zombies, Francis thought. Except the cold pressed against her and chased a shiver down her back, proving that she was still alive. A touch of blue peeked out from under her chipped black nail polish, creeping down into her fingers. The combination matched her mood; broken apart and held together by the cold in her heart.

"When's it starting?" she asked, aiming the question at whoever would answer.

"Gate's open," one reply came with an added lilt to each word. "Should be blood soon."

Twelve months ago, Francis would never have entertained the idea of spectating the rising. The sheer thought of people being eaten alive in front of her was one to stop her eating for a week and keep her light on every night. Her friends had seen the show before, and maintained that if they were going to be fed to the undead one day, then they would rather get used to the screams before it was their own assaulting their ears. Desensitising, some of them called it. They couldn't get their fix of death on the TV, thanks to government bans on all non-research related filming, but no one could stop them showing up at the cemetery walls. Even if some of those people were there simply to get off on the blood and death.

For Francis, it was neither a way to grow accustomed to the violence nor a way to get her kicks. All she wished for was a chance to see her father again. Eleven months he had been buried in the cemetery. The victim of a heart attack at an early age.

If she could just see him again, say goodbye, erase the last, teenage strop she'd had before he died…

When Sandra was a girl of five, she had gotten lost in this cemetery. Its maze-like walls had risen up around her as she ran, and the further she got, the higher the walls had seemed. Her great-grandmother was being buried, and Sandra had no clue about death or funerals. All she knew was that her wool coat itched and she was too warm on the autumn's day.

Zombie Lottery

The priest stood there prattling on about ashes and dust, and Sandra had slipped out of her mother's sobbing grasp and wandered off into the cemetery.

Three hours later, she was found curled up underneath a stone angel, fast asleep.

But before she had been found, Sandra had felt a lot like she did now. Remnants of things she didn't understand rising up around her. Death and fear towering above her and dripping down in an endless flood.

If only the silence of her childhood had visited with the torments of the present.

But the second she and Charlie got through the gates, the carnage and screams engulfed them. Already the paths were lined with the dead, both recent and risen. Chunks of flesh were scattered around in bloody masses that were unidentifiable. A couple of zombies still had bloody limbs dangling from their mouths as they tore people apart and chewed on the meat. Others were bent over screaming victims, clawing through clothes and into flesh. The screams burned as though acid was being poured into Sandra's ears. Yet the pain of continuous torture refused to fade, and every screech of someone being eaten alive burned anew.

Chaos reigned in the cramped space just inside the gates. Those unlucky enough to be first through had been mowed down by the eager dead.

Floodlights illuminated the blood and gore, highlighting every detail of the rotting corpses and fresh death. In the artificial day-bright cemetery blood gleamed against bone and puss oozed down greying skin.

At least the still-feeding dead were already preoccupied with their meals by the time Sandra and Charlie got to the gates. The pair raced past one man, still twitching as a zombie feasted on the flesh of his heart through torn-open ribs. Blood slopped around the chest cavity like dark tomato soup. Sandra suddenly regretted her dinner choice. She stumbled, hitting her knee on the edge of an old grave marker. What little was left in her forced its way up her throat and out her mouth. Her stomach clenched and her throat burned as she heaved. Panted breaths sent plumes of air up around her that mingled with the light steam rising from her regurgitated dinner.

"We've got to keep moving," Charlie urged.

Sandra's stomach disagreed and she retched again.

When she was done, she stayed kneeling in the wet grass, letting the cool refresh her overheated body.

Charlie tugged at her arm. She glanced up and followed his gaze to an approaching zombie. The grey man shuffled forwards at a deceptive pace. Everyone knew that they only appeared slow and stumbling when they were unfocused. One step unevenly in front of another was reserved for between meals. Once they spotted dinner, their uncoordinated shuffles took on the appearance of an athlete.

For now, the old man shuffled along at a steady speed. Charlie pulled at Sandra's arm until she got to her feet, wiping her mouth with the back of her hand as she did. He tugged her behind the gravestone she'd thrown up on. They crouched down as far as they could behind the broken stone.

Sandra held her breath. Her heart pounded. Her hands ran wet. But as her whole body shook with the effort to become invisible, Sandra couldn't help but wonder whether she was doing the right thing. Trying to survive came with the price of this night haunting her sleep for the rest of her life. Throwing herself to the undead granddad came with the price of this being over. Surely if she hurled herself at the thing, it would tear her throat out first and kill her quick.

Morbid hope for an easy death tickled Sandra's mind, made her fingers twitch, and had her shuffling her feet in the damp grass.

Zombie Lottery

Just as Sandra made up her mind to get it over with, the zombie spotted a meal and took off after it in a sprint.

Charlie sighed next to her.

"I almost gave up," Sandra whispered.

"What?"

"I thought about just throwing myself at the thing."

Charlie looked at her with narrow eyes. "Why didn't you?"

Sandra shrugged. "He ran away."

Charlie frowned for a moment then shrugged. His indifference to her desire to die came as a shock. For all his earlier talk of Sandra seeing her kids again, she got the impression he was more resigned to death than she was.

"We could do it," she offered.

"What, throw ourselves to the slaughter?"

"Why not? It's not like we can kill ourselves. That'd just get two more people thrown in here. And it isn't like they're going to feed us in ten hours when we're all cold and hungry."

Charlie chewed his lip for a moment. Then he straightened his back, squared his shoulders and shook his head. "No. I'd rather be cold and hungry with a chance that one of us gets out of here than dead without trying."

"And if we do survive? One of us goes home, and next year we get to sit at home waiting to see if our name gets drawn again. It's not winning if we survive. It's just an extension."

Still Charlie shook his head. "Another year with your kids? Another year where the scientists might solve this. No. We have to try."

Sandra smiled. "Then we better get lost."

She took Charlie's hand, then darted out and took off towards the centre of the cemetery.

~***~

From the surrounding wall of the cemetery, the spectators had a good view of the whole maze. Each of the central walls stood at ten feet high, but the outer walls were almost twenty in places. The cemetery had been built into the valley between three small hills, with the church it belonged to towering over the fourth wall. What once were the tops of rolling hills had long since been paved and turned into roads. The walls had been left in place to stop the land from caving in and engulfing the cemetery.

The original purpose of a maze being built in the middle of a cemetery was a mystery. Stories as to its origin and purpose abounded, and one lesson every year in Francis's history and English class was dedicated to those tales. Some said they had been part of an earlier, smaller cemetery that had eventually become the zombie filled maze.

The story that had fascinated Francis for almost a year, however, was the same tale behind the rusted bells and rotted strings that decorated some older graves.

The chances of anyone being buried alive now were so close to impossible that they ranked somewhere between a snowball in hell and the inferno freezing over. When the cemetery had been built, however, people had believed the dead could return. As such, walls were built to keep in the dead, and extras were added to confuse those within. Arranged in the form of a maze, the church had needed to put a map up at the entrance after a number of people got lost in there.

Little did the builders of those walls know that they would serve their intended purpose.

Francis had been ten years old when the first zombies came out of the ground. Most of the town's dead had been caught in the cemetery, wandering around behind the gates. Some, however, had been scattered in the woods or buried in shallow graves. It took three weeks for people to realise that once the dead were fed they went back to sleep.

Francis shook her head in an attempt to dislodge the cold that was distracting her. Below, several zombies were already shuffling back to their graves. Her friends crowded against the edge of the wall, placing hands on its edge and leaning in for a better view.

Smiles decorated their faces in spite of the screams that floated up around the place. Even their noses weren't wrinkled against the stench of bowels being torn open and rotting flesh.

Pushing her way past her friends, Francis made her way towards the wall for a better view. Where her friends laughed and pointed at the figures running for their lives, Francis stood still and quiet. She eyed every person she saw, zombie and alive alike. Hard to tell the difference when the undead ran.

With every figure she saw, the hope of seeing her father again faded. The more she lost hope, the colder she felt.

Having seen most of it more times than he wanted to remember, Jack didn't need to see the visual that went along with the screams. He had better things to do with his night. If he could, he would have worn earplugs and saved himself the memories of the screams, too.

His radio chirped to life, giving him a distraction.

"We got kids leaning over the wall. North corner."

Jack cursed. Every year those damn kids came to get their kicks. How they slept at night was beyond him.

He tugged his radio from the holder on his belt and thumbed the button. "Andy, you're up north, take a walk past, will ya?"

"Will do, boss."

The radio crackled for a second, then fell silent. Jack went back to his computer and the pictures his crew had taken. Everything on his laptop was organised into years. Once the pictures were sent over to the researchers, Jack took a look through them himself. Not for counting, but to see if he could see anything.

Sure, he didn't have the knowledge or training that the scientists had, but having been married to one briefly, he believed one thing wholeheartedly: scientists almost always over-complicated things.

So on the off chance that he could see a simple pattern, he poured over what he knew when he could. Unfortunately, he had yet to see anything other than a couple of repeat faces. Nothing that could be considered a pattern. Even the difference in numbers from year to year held nothing.

He flicked through the pictures again, squinting at each one as he scrolled through.

There's something here, he thought as another terrified scream made his heart clench. *There has to be something here.*

Hidden away in a specialist facility, Hannah opened her hundredth email of the night. She downloaded the attachments and placed them in a dated folder under the heading, Hinddale. Her facility was responsible for almost one hundred and fifty cemeteries. Once a year she received all the data each one could gather when the undead walked.

She compared each picture to the previous year's selection. Medical records, where available, were checked for any commonalities. But every single one was different. Deaths from heart failure, cancer, old age, accidents and even murder. Ages ranged from a few years old to the oldest person alive, or rather, dead. Gender and race played no part, either. It was like looking at a bunch of people gathered in one place the night before Christmas. Only common thing between them was that they were there.

Zombie Lottery

Hannah exhaled sharply and hit the escape key on her keyboard.

Every single year was the same, and yet she still hoped, still sent up a prayer for any kind of solution. She pushed her chair back, grabbed her lab coat, and headed down to the facility's graveyard. The wandering dead here were never given human life. They were dissected, cremated, fed animals, given donated blood, and even the occasional amputated limb, but never a life.

In the five long years Hannah had been working on the zombies, she knew almost everything about them. What she didn't know, was the one thing very much worth knowing; how to stop them rising. Or at the very least, how to stop them eating people.

Two of her colleagues were standing at the observation window that overlooked the graveyard. Calling it that was a stretch, however. Other than the dead ambling about, the stretch of land inside the building had no markers of a cemetery. No headstones or statues. No plants or flowers left by loved ones. The dead that were buried here had been done so with the sole purpose of studying them.

"How's the latest blood test going?" Hannah inquired.

"Nothing," Ian answered. "They're calmer than they were, but we sent Carl in with his suit on, and they went for him, soon as he made a noise." Ian shoved his hands deep into his pockets.

"Even with the damn earplugs we got into subject twelve, it went after me like a bat after dinner," Carl said.

Hannah shook her head and muttered, "We're running out of things to try."

"Yeah. 'Bout the most practical idea we've had is throwing them all in a pit and throwing blood at them from time to time."

Where to start with the flaws in that plan? Hannah thought. Not least of which being the practicality of housing millions of zombies.

The turned up corner of Ian's mouth caught Hannah's attention. It was his "guess what some idiot is thinking of trying," look.

"They're considering doing it? Aren't they?" She let her head fall back on her shoulders and cursed at the ceiling. "Sticking them all in a furnace was a better idea than that! At least it took a few weeks for the escaping ash to coalesce!"

Ian backed off a step, hands in the air. "I know, boss, I know that. But the policy makers are seeing millions die every year, and we got nothing."

Carl leaned against the room's reinforced glass window. "Shame this isn't some damn movie where we can shoot them in the head or blast them into space. Or, hell, infect ourselves with a bloody virus."

Hannah spun around so fast she nearly broke her neck. "What did you just say?"

Carl frowned.

Hannah marched over to him and shook his shoulders. "Say what you said again."

He repeated every word. Twice.

The smile on Hannah's face grew so wide her cheeks almost split.

"That's it! That's what we do!"

Before Ian or Carl had chance to ask what she was going on about, Hannah raced from the room muttering about solutions, her lab coat flying out behind her as she went.

"We've been running for hours," Sandra moaned as she and Charlie dodged another rotting zombie.

Charlie pulled her behind a wall, down past a mausoleum, and around another corner.

"It's been twenty minutes." He leaned back against the cold stone. "You don't run much, do you?"

Sandra bent over, hands on her knees as she panted. "Not unless you count chasing the kids. You clearly do."

"Park run, every weekend. Five kilometres, up and down hill." He shrugged.

Sandra collapsed to the floor and took a deep breath. If she had to keep running, she would be welcoming death in the end. And it wasn't like they had any weapons to give them a fighting chance. Running was their only option. Especially as blows to the head did little more than slow the zombies down for a while. Almost as though they were shaking off a concussion.

So many people had already given up and simply stood about until a zombie got them. That sight was what had changed Sandra's mind completely on the practice. One person, an older lady Sandra had spotted hiding behind a grave, had done exactly what Sandra had thought of doing. She rose up, steadying herself on the grave marker, and waited until the shuffling undead with its rotting face and arm got close. The woman did exactly what Sandra wanted to do; threw herself at the undead hard and fast, giving herself no time to change her mind.

Except that the zombie hadn't gone at the woman's throat. The force of the old woman knocked the pair of them to the floor with a thud. First bite landed on the woman's shoulder, far enough away from her throat that she could still scream whilst she was eaten alive. Blood and puss blended together as the zombie wrapped its rotting arm around her bleeding shoulders.

With that image lodged in her mind, Sandra lost the appeal of throwing herself to her death in the hopes it would be quick.

"How many do you think are left?" she asked. "There's got to be less than half, right?"

Charlie shrugged. "If you want me to get technical about our chances, I'd bore you to death before the zombies got you."

Sandra laughed, a short sound that ended in a cough.

"My day job is statistics," Charlie explained. "And once a year, I get to write up the survival and winning stats for the lottery."

As cold as the night was, Sandra still felt every ounce of her blood drain from her face. Stood in front of her was a man who knew exactly what the odds were of either of them getting out alive.

Charlie's eyes were drawn tight, the corner of his lips curled into a harsh smile.

"Come on," he said after a moment of tense silence, "let's see if we can screw up my statistics!"

Cheers and screams mingled in the air around Francis. Below, the ground was painted with splashes of red, severed limbs, and zombies digging themselves back into their graves. Flesh was nothing new. Though dissecting a frog up close involved a lot less mess than seeing the undead rip off the leg of someone trying to escape.

Around her, Francis's friends were huddled close together, sharing blankets and passing around cheap bottles of booze. A couple of the blankets moved with their occupants as they got hot and heavy at the sight of death.

Sex, Francis was fond of, but how the sights, sounds, and smells of the dying could be considered foreplay was beyond her. She didn't see fucking in the eating of flesh or making love in the sighs of relief when the zombies were done and ready to sleep.

That's how her friends described it. Arousal in the face of death. Sexual attraction whilst they still could.

A couple more years, and they would all be included in the lottery. Any of them could be called up and escorted to the cemetery. Some of them already were.

Personally, Francis thought they were all either sick or sheep. Following the herd because it was the in thing to do, because everyone else was doing it.

Those around her getting off on it couldn't be anything but sick.

With a sigh, Francis rubbed her hands together and stamped her feet. She peered down into the cemetery. Somewhere down there, either dead or undead, was her father.

A figure stumbled around the dividing wall directly below her. Tattered black pants dragged on the floor where they were too long. The shirt and jacket flapped in a wind that whipped around the wall. Dead eyes in a rotting face stared into nothing, seeing nothing.

Francis gasped as those dead eyes swung up to the cheering group at the wall.

Somewhere deep in her mind, she knew he wasn't seeing her, but that didn't stop her gripping the wall and leaning over as far as she could.

"Dad!" she shouted. Her cry was swallowed in the cheer of her friends as her undead father rushed the wall and scrambled for the live meat making so much noise.

Carl and Ian had both followed Hannah back to her office. Neither said a word as she tore through her files, a constant prayer falling from her lips.

"Can we help?" Carl asked in a small voice.

Hannah didn't even look up when she replied. "At the moment, yes. Stay out of my way."

The smile that decorated her face was evident in her voice, and the two men backed as far away as the door. They stayed there, however, and Hannah was fine with that. If this worked—and all her fingers and toes were crossed—then tonight would be the last zombie rising they ever saw.

The file that she was after found her fingers as if it has been searching for her just as hard as she was for it. She grabbed the folder, tore it open, and yanked out the papers within. Taking them over to her desk, Hannah spread the sheets out and beckoned Carl and Ian from the doorway.

"Take a stack," she ordered. "These are the notes from the immunisation trials. I know they didn't work, but I want to know if anyone tried injecting the zombies."

"Not the humans?"

She turned to the two men, eyes sparkling. "Exactly. We're been trying to stop people from rising or trying to send the zombies back to sleep. But what if we inject something into the zombie once it's risen? No one's tried that, I don't think. So look through these, and hurry. If it's not been done before, then I want to try it in lab and non-lab conditions. Tonight."

Blood sprayed out, hot in the cold night. It covered Charlie's face and stained his pale jacket. The jacket pissed him off more than the blood in his eyes and mouth. He'd had the jacket on order for three months before it finally arrived a month ago. His irritation soon passed. After all, it was his own damn fault for wearing it on lottery night.

Beside him, Sandra threw up again. He couldn't decide what was worse; the dead person all over the floor and him, or the stench of bile. Whatever Sandra's last meal had been had long since been puked out onto the cemetery's ground. All she had left was bile that matched the puss oozing out of every zombie they evaded.

At least her vomiting did nothing to attract the already feasting undead. Sandra continued to retch, and morbid curiosity got the better of Charlie. Everyone alive had seen pictures and news footage depicting the annual rising, but relatively few got to see the walking dead up close and really appreciate it.

The shambling dead in front of him was everything the news had portrayed it to be. Skin that had once been vibrant was now grey with a blue edge, complete with green puss oozing from various tears in the flesh. Charlie thought it was as though whatever brought them back only got partly done reanimating them before giving up.

Sandra wiped her mouth, and looked up at him. "How come you're not throwing your guts up?"

He shrugged, then realised that explained nothing. "When I do the stats, it comes with full colour pictures. Up close, it ain't much different. Smellier, yes, and much greater detail, but not all that different."

Which was a lie. In person, seeing people ripped apart should have been harrowing. Sure, the sight of half eaten bodies was exactly like he'd seen, but how they got that way came with a whole different range of sights, smells, and sounds. Thankfully, the cold air muted a lot of the smells. The screams, however, did little to mask the sound of arms being ripped from their sockets and chests being torn open, one rib at a time.

Charlie glanced over to the dead body sprawled out on someone's grave. The zombie, a young looking woman with long flowing hair, crouched over the flesh, feasting on the ribs and heart as though she hadn't seen food in weeks.

Hell, maybe they come back because the afterlife is short on food, Charlie thought.

He had done the same with his food after a long day at work where he had woken up too late for breakfast and missed lunch. Chicken for dinner had seen him doing exactly what the zombie was doing; tearing into his food with his fingers and pulling out chunks of hot meat and shovelling it into his mouth.

Like Charlie on that particular meal, the zombie's whole demeanour was focused on the meal in front of her. So much so that even Charlie and Sandra standing ten feet away made no impression.

Charlie averted his eyes. He might not have been revisiting his dinner like Sandra, but he didn't much like the visual comparison.

"How much longer do you think we need to keep this up?" Charlie asked.

A shuffling behind them turned both their heads in unison. The low moaning emanated from several throats. A zombie rounded the corner. The pair's eyes went wide as a second and third undead followed the first.

Charlie cursed. He reached for Sandra's arm and dragged her up. The group spotted them, their whole bodies shifting from uninterested to alert in an instant.

As Charlie dragged Sandra into a run, the zombies followed. Their limbs may have appeared half finished and weak but they ran better than most of the living.

Charlie's heart pounded in his chest. The combination of fear and exhaustion making it beat so hard he thought it would burst free and save him the pain of being eaten. His breathing laboured and his feet slapped against the cold earth.

As he ran, he scanned the cemetery in front of him. Walls and monuments rose all around them. Most were undisturbed, but some had huge piles of dirt scattered around where the zombies had crawled free.

The pair dodged and weaved their way through the maze, tripping and stumbling as they went. A wall loomed ahead of them.

"There!" Charlie shouted, unable to control the volume of his voice.

He dragged Sandra towards the wall, skidded as he pulled her around it, and righted himself just in time to see another zombie in front of them.

"There's nothing in here," Carl said, slapping his pile of papers on the desk.

Hannah looked up from her stack, separated what was left, and handed it to Carl. She tapped her foot against the bar on her desk, trying to contain the hope that threatened to make her heart soar. The lower the number of pages dropped, the more she wanted to rush through them in the hopes of being right.

Such a stupid idea, she thought. But if it worked…

"Done," Ian said. He leaned back in his chair and stretched. "Nothing in here, either."

Hannah flicked through her remaining pages but didn't split them down again.

She scanned every word of every page, searching for those few key words that would bring her idea crashing down. The word injection leapt off the page and slapped her in the face. She almost swore. This was the umpteenth time, however, that she had seen the word, and knew to read deeper before letting her heart stop completely.

"Injection into subject ten, five hours after death."

She sighed in relief. Every injection she had read about so far had been done on a living human or dead, unrisen body. Nothing on a zombie that had clawed its way free from the grave.

The last page was free from any of the trigger words she had been looking for.

"Is that it?" she asked. "Is that all the trials?"

Carl set his last sheet aside and glanced around the room. Piles of papers were sat on every available surface, piled high on the floor, and teetering on the edge of the desk. "That's the last of them."

Which was a blessing in itself. After going through the initial file stack, Hannah had wanted to cover all the angles and go through every file they had. Just in case.

Ian cracked his neck, stretched, and leaned forward. "You want to tell us why we just spent three hours going over every trial we have?"

Hannah sat back in her chair and kicked away from the desk,

knocking a stack of papers over in the process.

"We've been injecting the dead and dying."

Carl frowned. "Yeah. Who else are we supposed to inject?"

A wide grin spread across Hannah's face as she answered, "The zombies."

Jack's radio crackled to life and Andy's voice shouted out. "We got one over the wall! Someone jumped over the fucking wall!"

Jack sprang from his chair and was reaching for his radio when Andy added, "She jumped into the cemetery! Just jumped right over the god damned wall."

He froze, one hand on the radio. With slow, precise movements, Jack brought the handset up and clicked the button. "Say again, Andy. Someone jumped *in* to the cemetery?"

Once upon a time a zombie had made it out of the cemetery during the rising. Jack and his crew had reacted quick enough, putting enough bullets in it to slow the thing down long enough to get it back in the cemetery. Such events, though rare, were the reason all his crew members were licenced and trained to carry firearms. No one, however, in the entire history of the lottery, had jumped the wall. Not willingly.

Andy must have meant that one of those damn groupie kids had fallen in, having gotten too close to the wall.

"She jumped in!" he shouted over the radio. "Jumped right the fuck on in."

This was an unprecedented situation. The crew kept an eye on those at the wall, but to stop people *falling* in, not jumping.

Jack bolted past his chair, catching it on his hip and knocking it to the floor with a clatter.

"I'll get the ladder," he called. "Everyone else, night's not over. Stay on task." No sense letting the whole thing get out of hand because of one stupid kid with a death wish.

He raced to his van, and nimbly released the ladders from the rack on top. It took him a moment to get the length situated on his shoulders before he took off running for the north corner.

"Out of the way!" he shouted as he ran.

People scattered away from the wall. Some tripped and fell and were dragged out of the way by others. Jack's feet punched at the ground. The long ladders rattled in protest at their harsh transport.

Andy's tall, bulky frame was easily spotted amongst the teenagers. He had them backed away from the wall, giving Jack enough room to manoeuvre the ladders off his shoulders.

"What happened?" Though he didn't need to ask. From this side of the wall, Jack had a perfect view of what was going on below, as unbelievable as it was.

Some days, Hannah thought her protective gear weighed more than she did. It looked like a modern suit of armour. Instead of heavy silver lined with chainmail covering every inch of her, the suit was made up of lightweight, black materials. Their facility had three such suits, and they were all in use now.

Hannah had long since lost count of times a zombie had tried to bite her through the gear. None had ever managed more than a scratch, and if the idea had been viable, the whole world would be wearing suits full time. But battling zombies down the high street was too much added stress for the shoppers, not to mention the expense of a single suit running into the thousands of pounds.

Hannah fastened the last black buckle in place and strapped on her glove. Before she was allowed in the cemetery, her whole body had to be covered from head to foot. Hanging at her side was a canvas bag in matching black. Carl and Ian wore the same gear.

Inside their bags were pre-loaded syringes filled with several different compounds. The heavy gauge apparatus had been specifically designed for use with the suits. Standard needles were too fine and required the motor skills of latex not armour.

"Let's do this," Hannah said over the built in comms.

The trio entered the antechamber that separated them from the undead. The only entryway had a secure double door system. Only one door at any time could be opened, thus preventing their year-round crop of zombies from escaping.

It took several seconds for the door behind them to ease shut and click into place. A backlit number panel illuminated once one door was locked, and Hannah punched the code into the large numbered keypad. The door swung open on silent hinges. They entered in a quick and orderly fashion, just like they did every time they all went in.

To get out again, they each needed their own code and a full body scan to make sure they were alive, not undead.

"Pick a number, boys," Hannah said. "I've got subject three."

Ian said, "I'll take seven."

"I got fourteen."

Before they split off, they each got out an injection and compared details. Out of the five options they had, they wanted to do them in order, make sure they got the same results from the same thing. Once confirmed, they each set off for their chosen undead, syringe in hand.

Hannah got to hers first, and before the thing could react to her presence, she stuck her needle in its dirt and puss covered neck and backed away.

Her mask threatened to steam up as her breathing increased. She forced herself to stop, take a breath, and back away more slowly. No matter how often she came face to face with one of the zombies, her heart rate always tried to climb for the roof.

The zombie took a step towards her, and Hannah held her breath. In her mind, a prayer took root. She repeated the words of hope over and over, not for her own life, which was pretty secure in the suit, but for all the lives this idea could save.

The zombie took a second, unsteady step. It reached for Hannah with a rotting arm that dripped green.

"Come on," Hannah whispered, unable to hold her breath any longer.

As the undead approached, she slipped a hand into her bag. The front pocket held several bags of human blood. It wouldn't stop the creature, but it would slow it down long enough to move on to another subject.

"It's not working!" came the call over the radio from Carl.

Hannah didn't hesitate. She tore the top off the bag of blood and flung it in the zombie's face. Bright red sprayed the creature's face and dripped down, mingling with puss. In a second, its attention shifted from Hannah to the blood.

Carl and Ian called out their next subject numbers, Hannah did the same, and the three confirmed which syringe they were using next.

Which got them exactly the same results as the first. And the same again for their third try.

With only two left, Hannah was beginning to think she was heading down the wrong path. Again.

Still, she thought, *two left, might as well give it a go.*

"I've got twenty-seven," she informed the guys. They came back straight away with their subject numbers, and they began the experiment again. By four shots in, they were all familiar with the process. Voices confirmed the next injection to be given.

Hannah came up behind her tagged zombie and stuck the needle in its neck before it even knew there was a meal standing there.

33

The undead man, dressed in clothes that had to be a hundred years old or more, jerked when the needle went in. For half a heartbeat, Hannah thought she might have to run again. Her heart rate spiked, her muscles tensed, and her hand slipped into her back and rested on another bag of blood.

It turned, lifted its arm… and fell flat on its face with a squelch.

"Are they dead?" Ian asked over the radio. "Did we just solve this mess?"

Hannah's heart now pounded for a different reason, but she said, "Give it a minute."

They waited in silence. A minute passed. Then five more. Subject twenty-seven stayed face down in the dirt.

Slowly, Hannah bent down and gripped the zombie's shoulders. With a heave, she turned it over. The chunk of her gloves hindered her, but she didn't dare take them off, so she struggled to pry the zombie's eyes open.

Puss made it hard to grip and harder to see. Its eyes were unresponsive to light. If she had to guess, Hannah would have said she was staring at a dead body.

"I think it worked," she said, her voice barely above a breath. "I think we did it!"

The only question that remained was whether they had solved the whole mess, or just put a hold on it for a while.

If Sandra had been given the choice between life and death, in the second she and Charlie rounded the corner, she would have chosen death. And she would have been wrong.

From everything she had ever seen or heard, when something bad happened, it all happened so quickly. Everything became a blur and couldn't possibly be recounted in detail. But as she rounded the corner, every single thing in that moment became etched in perfect detail onto her mind.

The three zombies behind them were matching Sandra and Charlie for speed. Moss covered the wall that rose up in front of them. Charlie's grip on Sandra's arm shifted as he steered them in that direction. A gravestone so old the name had long since weathered away stood at the edge of the wall. The plan, so Sandra thought, was to duck behind the grave and hope the zombies passed them by in the heat of the chase.

But as Sandra skidded around the grave and prepared to duck, another zombie appeared as if from nowhere.

The dark haired man stood by the retaining wall, hands still poised in a scramble towards what Sandra wanted most; freedom. Sandra cursed before she could stop the words falling from her lips. The zombie turned. Sandra cursed again. Didn't matter that the zombies behind her would have gotten its attention regardless.

Three behind. One in front. Suddenly, not praying for solutions seemed like an awful waste of time.

Whoever was watching out for Sandra and Charlie, however, must have appreciated the lack of disturbance. A girl, no older than sixteen or seventeen, leapt over the wall and right into the cemetery.

Shouts of alarm followed her fall. People leaned over the top, arms outstretched as though they could still catch her.

With her mind still seeing everything in crystal clear clarity, Sandra didn't hesitate in taking over where Charlie froze in shock. She grabbed his arm and hauled him behind the gravestone as planned.

He unfroze long enough to say, "We've got to help her!"

"We're supposed to be trying to survive, not risking our life over someone else." Sandra winced as she realised the harshness of her words. The lottery, however, was in its fifth year now, and she couldn't afford to have a heart, not if it meant the difference between getting out alive and ending up dead. Tomorrow she would feel guilty.

Sandra sat up and peered over the edge of the headstone she and Charlie were hidden behind. The three zombies that had been behind them were in the middle of a melee over the girl. The other zombie appeared to be winning, but as limbs flew and puss dripped, the fight continued.

Even when the unbelievable happened, no matter how focused on the zombie fight Sandra was there was no way she could miss the ladder that descended over the wall of the cemetery.

Her breath quickened and caught in her throat as her heart fought to break free. For the first time since her name had been drawn in the lottery, Sandra felt hope.

"We can get out," she whispered. "If we can get to that ladder, we can get out."

Never before had a set of simple stairs caused so much excitement. So much, in fact, that Sandra could have sworn they were glowing.

"You need your suit!" Andy shouted as Jack heaved the ladder over the wall. "You'll get yourself killed, damn it!"

Jack glanced over his shoulder. "You think she's got time for me to get my suit on? I'm going in."

He swung a leg over the wall and planted his work boot on the top rung. As soon as his second boot was on the ladder, he said to Andy, "No one in or out. Keep everyone back. And for God's sake, if one of them tries to get out, don't let it."

He took the rungs down as quick as he could, thankful the ground under him was soft enough that the ladder sunk in and steadied itself. The noise of the thing wasn't anything he could help, and no doubt it would draw more zombies, but as long as he got in and out quick, he hoped it would be all right.

Andy was right, though; he should have gotten his suit.

Jack hit the ground, turned, and wished like hell he had more than stale blood to ward off the undead. A flamethrower would have helped. Maybe a machine gun. But both of those would have killed the person he was trying to save.

If I can still save her, he thought.

Some miracle might have occurred in the crush of living dead he approached, but until he got most of the zombies off, he wouldn't know either way.

He grabbed three bags of blood from his bag. One in each hand and one in his teeth. They fit his large hands with ease, and he tore the tops open with practiced movement. Seconds later, he tossed two packets of blood over the fighting group, tore open the third with his teeth, and added it to the sloppy mess.

Two of the zombies broke away. The third came slower. The fourth was too busy eating.

No thoughts of broken legs or death entered Francis' mind when she spotted her dad. Before anyone could stop her, and even before her own mind could chime in with the downsides of her plan, she leapt over the wall. Air rushed past her for a brief moment before she hit the ground and rolled. When she stopped, she lay there for a moment, oblivious to the commotion above her.

Whilst she was still panting, she pushed against the cold ground and forced her body to its feet. Her limbs moved as though the fall had turned her into one of the shambling dead.

"Dad!" she cried.

The zombie that was her father turned. It took one shambling step forwards. Then another. Then it closed the distance in a run and threw its arms around her.

Francis sobbed. "I love you, Dad. I'm so sorry for everything I said."

Words continued to tumble from her lips until they were cut short by the pain that lanced through her shoulder. Three other zombies knocked her and her father down to the grass. The addition was both a blessing and a curse. Had her father been able to sink his teeth into her shoulder, it would be over. Not instantly, and not for a while. But the alternative was four undead tearing her apart until one got its teeth into her. Francis paid little attention to what her death would be like. She was with her father.

Yet as the commotion continued and the screams of alarm finally reached her ears, something crossed her mind.

Funny, she thought, *they were all getting off on the gore before.* But she'd figured her friends were fickle enough to enjoy the suffering of others when it had no effect on them.

Something cold hit Francis' face, and her first thought was that it wasn't supposed to rain tonight.

"I'm sorry, Dad," she said again.

When the pain hit this time, it didn't stop. Dull edged teeth forced their way into her shoulder. Pain stopped her words long enough to let a scream loose. Her mantra soon began again as more rain soaked her hair and face.

Hannah dialled a number she had no right calling. If her ex-husband didn't answer, it would serve her right for what she did to him. No amount of apologies could change the fact that he had walked in on her in bed with his best friend. The phone went to voicemail.

"Listen, Jack, I'm going to keep trying. If you get this, call me. I know how to end this mess. Zombies. Not us."

Next message she had to leave, she planned on starting with the zombies. At least then he might be less likely to just delete the messages without listening.

If she could have gone anywhere else, she would have, but they needed non-lab conditions. They needed zombies that hadn't been tested with anything else and no residual effects from previous experiments. And they needed it now. Tonight. Before they had to wait another year to see if they had fixed the issue.

She was well aware that the chances three randomly picked zombies having the exact same reaction thanks to previous tests were slim. Slim, however, was still a chance, no matter how unlikely.

"Can we drive faster?" Hannah asked.

"Not with these damned suits on," Ian snapped. He shook his head. "Sorry. We're five minutes away."

Hannah dialled Jack's phone again.

"Do you really think they're going to just let us walk away?" Charlie asked with a shake of his head.

Tempting as the ladder to freedom was, he was under no illusions that if they made it to the wall, they would get up the ladder. But then what? Wander back to their lives and continue as normal? Did Sandra really think that was an option?

"No," he said. "Best bet is to outlast everyone. That girl is dead. So there's two chances of not dying, right?"

Sandra's attention was focused on the ladder. Her hands gripped the edge of the crumbling grave stone. Charlie had to shake her shoulder.

"Look, they're not just going to let us walk," he said again.

She finally turned to him, her eyes alight with determination.

Charlie shook her shoulders again. "Are you listening?"

She glanced back to the ladder. "The zombies are distracted. We can go now."

"You're not hearing me. They are not going to let us just walk away."

"They might," she whispered.

"No." Charlie sighed deeply. "If you want to try, I'm not going to stop you. But I think you're stupid if you honestly think you can walk back into your life like this."

He turned away from her and sat with his back against the cold stone. With only so many ways he could phrase the word "no," he was fast running out of them.

Damned woman's delusional, he thought.

Hope was also what he saw in her eyes, but hope and delusion often went together. Didn't mean either of them were bad, just that the combination often led to stupidity. With the dead above ground and wanting blood, stupid was synonymous with dead.

"I'm going for it," Sandra said. "Whilst they're distracted."

Charlie waved a hand in dismissal. He wanted to survive. Survival, in his mind, did not go well with being on the run for the rest of his life. The pact he and Sandra made to keep each other alive came to mind. It didn't change his mind about her stupidity, but it did make him curious about her outcome. He rose to his knees, and peered over the edge of the gravestone.

Sandra's shoulders lifted as she took a deep breath. He saw her legs tense, but as she was about to make a run for it, sirens filled the air. Seconds later, the cemetery was bathed in flashing red and blue lights.

Sandra ducked back down and cursed.

"How did they know?" she cried.

Charlie looked for the source of the light. Three figures in armoured suits appeared at the top of the wall. One by one, they descended the ladder. Charlie glanced back at Sandra. "I don't think they're here for you."

~***~

Jack cursed. She was just a kid. Shouldn't have even been out here. She wasn't dead yet, either, but he knew all too well that without a cure, there was no saving her. Even if the zombie had started with her feet, there would be no stopping it.

His phone buzzed on his belt, and he cursed. Whoever it was could wait.

Best Jack could do now was give the poor girl a quick death. In the bottom of his bag sat a hammer that was used in the rare event that the blood pacifier wore off too quickly. Blows to the head worked well enough if all you wanted to do was get away. Worked well on humans, too. His fingers closed around the well-worn wooden handle just as sirens pierced the night.

He spun towards the sound. No matter how many people called the emergency services tonight none of them would come close to the cemetery. Jack and his team were the emergency services. Only in the event that they lost control would the reinforcements be brought in.

A black Land Rover pulled right up to the wall, and two figures emerged from one side. Jack recognised one of them.

All thoughts of giving the girl a quick death vanished from Jack's mind as his feet took him over to the ladder.

Before he could get one foot on the thing, a pair of boots appeared over the top of the wall. Added weight from the guy's suit made the ladder sway. Jack grabbed it with both fists clenched tight and one boot planted on the bottom rung. He stepped to the side when the first guy got close enough to the ground. Soon as the first one was down, he grabbed the ladder again as the second came down. Then the third.

Only one thing was going through Jack's mind, and it had nothing to do with his ex-wife standing in front of him decked out in lab-grade zombie gear.

Only reason she would be anywhere near him was if she had

something to end this mess.

"Do it," he said in a gruff voice. "I don't care what it is, just do it."

Sandra hit the ground with a curse so loud it should have attracted every zombie in the place.

That ladder was her one chance to get back to her family. And if living meant being on the run with her kids forever, then there was no choice, no question.

She looked up at Charlie with eyes that were shiny with tears. "What are we going to do?"

Her question wasn't directed at him in particular, he just happened to be there. She would have taken an answer from anyone.

The answer she received, however, had nothing and everything to do with what she wanted.

"Hey, look! They're sending guys in."

Sandra shook her head and a tear spilled onto her cheek.

Charlie cursed, but where the words had been desperate from Sandra, they sounded excited from Charlie. "They dropped the zombie!"

Sandra sniffled, replayed his words twice, wiped her eyes, and peered over the edge of the moss covered stone… just in time to see two people in zombie gear high five each other. A third approached the group of undead that had been fighting over the girl. A syringe went into neck after neck, and seconds later, the zombies flopped to the ground in a pile of puss covered limbs.

They're found a cure, Sandra thought, and the voice in her mind was joyous.

She reached for Charlie's hand and grinned. "Looks like we're going home."

~***~

Zombie Lottery

It worked, Hannah thought with glee. As the third zombie hit the floor within a second of being injected there wasn't a thing in the world that could have made her happier. She checked that they were out before reaching up and removing her helmet. The cemetery wasn't empty, she knew that, but in order to get to the rest of them she needed Jack's help. Her knowledge of this cemetery was limited to its size, location, and the undead that rose every year.

The thought of her ex took her joy down a notch. As she strode back to Ian, Carl, and Jack, Hannah kept her head high. The issues she and Jack had were nothing to do with the evening. Saving lives was on the agenda, not her screwing up their marriage.

Ian was knelt on the ground next to the zombie he had injected. Laid on the floor next to it was a very dead girl. Her whole throat had been torn open, exposing her collarbone to the bright lights of their still running Land Rover.

"She's gone," Ian confirmed.

Jack stamped a foot and planted his hands on his hips. The gesture was one Hannah was familiar with, and meant he had been within the walls trying to save the girl.

"Damn girl jumped over the wall. She's not old enough to be picked. All she kept saying was sorry, over and over." He sighed and shook his head. "Kept calling it dad."

Hannah didn't think she would get a better chance than playing on Jack's obvious feeling of guilt to get the help she needed.

"How many more are still alive?" she asked. "We brought enough injections for at least half."

Jack looked up from the floor and glared at Hannah. Seconds later, his glare softened to a simple stare.

"This put them out for good?"

Hannah took a deep breath. "We don't know."

"But it'll work for tonight?"

"This is the test run." She pursed her lips and blew out a breath. "There's no way to tell. Not yet—"

"But it doesn't matter," Carl cut in. "Even if we have to shoot them up every six months, it doesn't matter. It buys us the time we need to fix this for good."

Jack nodded once and reached for his radio. "Listen up, everyone. I want all spectators out of here. Now. Those of you with suits, get them on. All hands on deck. It's time we ended this shit."

For the first time since before her divorce, Hannah saw Jack smile, a full blown, cheek splitting grin.

Whole hours could have passed as Charlie and Sandra stood behind the gravestone before anyone noticed them. The big guy without a suit spotted them and jogged over.

A smile lit up his face. "Looks like it's your lucky night," he said in a low voice.

Sandra's whole body vibrated with suppressed excitement. "I can go home?" She didn't dare raise her voice above a whisper in case it was all a dream and the mere sound brought it all crashing down.

The man shook his head. "You can get out, but we need to debrief you before you can leave."

Sandra's knees turned to jelly, and if it wasn't for Charlie, she would have ended up on the ground in a heap.

Despite being told they could leave, however, both Sandra and Charlie stayed where they were. Disbelief rooted them to the spot and froze their bodies in place.

"Go!" the guy said. "Not many people walk away from this."

Sandra's mind was so blank for a moment that all she could do was blink. Then a million thoughts danced across her mind. Birthdays still to come. Nights alone with her husband. Even arguments she couldn't wait to have. It was as though her whole life was flashing before her eyes, but the life that she had yet to live, not the life she had already seen.

She threw her arms around Charlie, and thought she heard a bone crack in the process.

The pair of them then ran for the ladder and began the climb that led to the rest of their lives.

If Sandra had thought the ladder shone like a beacon of hope before, now the metal gleamed, and in its shiny surface she saw reflected back at her all the hopes and dreams she had thought she would never live to see.

Acknowledgements

To the wonderful people who helped with this book. Chris, to whom this book is dedicated. Without you, there wouldn't be a book. There also wouldn't have been the incident with me suddenly being in the middle of Urban Outfitters wondering what planet I was on. However, I can't blame you entirely. I was the one who decided to write whilst walking.

Alice and Amy for editing. You may, one day, be my editing duo. I may also be able to pay you more than free books for your tireless efforts to make me sound better.

Also, to my husband. Who, despite my promise that this was all over and there would be no more pages, dutifully sat down and read through this entire story one morning. I can't thank you enough, so hopefully the occasional coffee and a constant supply of games will do.

And lastly, to everyone who comes back and reads more of my books no matter how often I produce them. You guys all rock.

About Michelle Birbeck

Michelle has been reading and writing her whole life. Her earliest memory of books was when she was five and decided to try and teach her fish how to read, by putting her Beatrix Potter books *in* the fish tank with them. Since then her love of books has grown, and now she is writing her own and looking forward to seeing them on her shelves, though they won't be going anywhere near the fish tank.

You can find more information on twitter, Facebook, and her website:

Facebook.com/MichelleBirbeck
Twitter: @michellebirbeck
www.michellebirbeck.co.uk

Books by Michelle Birbeck

The Keepers' Chronicles
The Last Keeper (Book 1)
Last Chance (Book 2)
Exposure (Book 3)
Revelations (Book 4)
A Glimpse Into Darkness (A Keepers' Chronicles short story)

Other Novels

The Stars Are Falling

Short Stories
The Phantom Hour
Consequences
Playthings
Zombie Lottery
Short Story compilation:
The Perfect Gift
Isolation
Never Go There
Survival Instincts